It's Just **Better** When You Do It **Together**

JENNETTE MIDGETT SOCKWELL
Illustrated by Kimberly Merritt

ISBN 978-1-7374490-0-3 (paperback) 978-1-7374490-1-0 (hardback)

Editing, formatting, cover, and illustrations by ChristianEditingandDesign.com.

To my mother, Carolyn, and her father,
William Ralph Gwaltney—Grandaddy G

The puppy
felt a surge of joy
and knew he'd found true love.
As they drove the long way home,
he watched the clouds above.

The happy puppy
fell asleep and knew
he'd found his place.
The people who would care for him
would also keep him safe.

He dreamed
of happy days to come
and friends he'd surely meet.
He dreamed of belly rubs and hugs,
and obviously treats!

When the puppy
woke next morning,
warm in bed with balls and toys,
his little tail wagged joyfully
because he heard a noise.

Feeling very brave and smart,
he jumped up quick to see:
His people sitting
next to him, singing
"Welcome home, Derby!"

Derby's tail wagged quickly
when he heard them
say his name,
because he knew that from now on,
everything would change!

His family loved him
very much, and every day
they'd play.
He'd go on grand adventures
and he'd learn along the way!

Derby hopes you'll come along
and watch him as he grows.
He'll make new friends
and try new things,
and learn to use his nose!

Be on the
lookout!
More adventures
with Derby
are on the way!

Made in the USA
Monee, IL
17 April 2021

Granddaddy G was my mother's father. And as far back as I can remember, Granddaddy G would say,

"It's just better when you do it together."

There were only two children in my family—me and my sister Jenifer. We have always been super close, but when we were little girls, sometimes we'd get in an argument and fight. We even pulled each other's hair. But it didn't take long before one of us was sorry. We'd tuck little apology notes under our bedroom door.

Our mother was an only child. She often reminded us that a sister is a treasured friend. She even shared that when she was a little girl, she "wished on a star" for a baby sister. So, she'd play with her cousins and friends. Granddaddy G would drive them everywhere and they'd hear him say, "It's just better when you do it together."

Granddaddy G cherished his daughter, whom he called "Little Carolyn." She was the apple of his eye and everyone knew it. And when my mother had two little girls of her own, he cherished us, too. Granddaddy G showed us that no matter what we were doing—*It's just better when you do it together.*

Granddaddy G was steady as a rock. Nothing seemed to upset him. People were drawn to his big smile and friendly personality. It didn't matter where we went. He never met a stranger. Whether we were on a road trip to a state park picnic, a store to buy Goo-Goo Clusters and Chunky candy bars, or the Farmers' Market to buy peaches, Granddaddy G would be talking and connecting with people.

He'd introduce us to everyone he met. He was a living example of kindness. As we were leaving his new friends, he'd say, "Goodbye. The girls and I must run more errands."

Then he'd whisper in his sweet, humble voice, and we'd hear those special words, "'It's just better when you do it together."' .

Visits to my grandparents' home, even just the ordinary and doing normal stuff visits, are now the shining stars of my childhood. They are my bright and sparkling memories. Granddaddy G and Grandmama never minded if we slept in late and stayed in our pajamas until lunch, but they did believe making our bed was an important routine. Each morning Granddaddy G would call, "Girls, come in here and let's make up this bed." He'd stand on one side of the bed, holding the sheet and bedspread, and we would grab the other side and in two or three pulls, the bed was made. We placed decorative pillows on the bed like sprinkles on top of a cupcake. Granddaddy G would chuckle and say,

Granddaddy G loved helping Grandmama every chance he could. Grandmama was an excellent cook. However, the mess of preparing the meals took the fun out of cooking for her. All through their house you could smell the wonderful aromas of her delicious casseroles and homemade rolls baking. But Grandmama was keenly aware of the sink full of dirty mixing bowls, spatulas, and spoons. Like a slow leak in a helium party balloon, the stress of the mess could easily suck the joy out of the room. So, Granddaddy G would stand at the sink with a rag in hand and wash those dirty dishes in hot, soapy water. He'd call for us: "Come in here and dry these dishes, girls. It's just better when you do it together."

Granddaddy G loved to feed us fruit. He never asked if we wanted a snack. He just knew we'd gobble it up. We'd be watching TV and almost magically a yellow bowl of peeled apples, sliced pears, and juicy peaches would appear on the coffee table or the couch cushion. We'd all lounge in the den, mindlessly snacking on the pieces of fruit while watching TV. Granddaddy G smiled and said,

"'It's just better when you do it together."

Before long it was dinner time. Grandmama always set a beautiful table with her special dinnerware. A green-trimmed dinner plate was surrounded by a fork and napkin on the left and a knife and spoon on the right. She used fresh-cut buttercups or irises in the prettiest little antique vase for a centerpiece, or sometimes a plastic tea glass. And she would never forget the butter dish and butter knife.

Granddaddy G always wanted us to be good helpers. He'd say, "Come set the table for Grandmama, girls." And of course, it wouldn't take much time at all because Granddaddy's words were true—

"It's just better when you do it together."

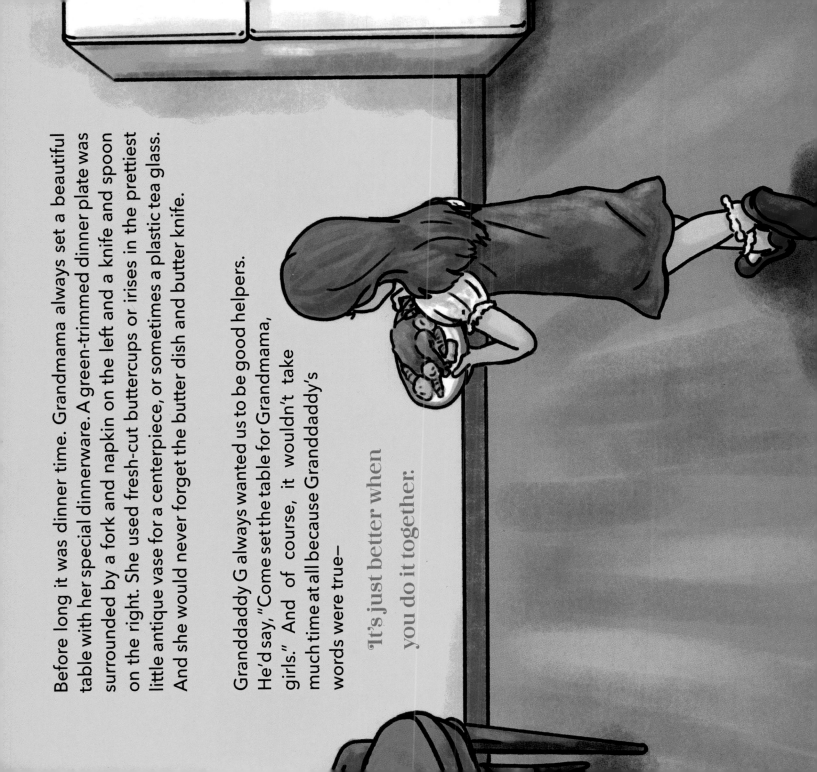

Life was always sweeter when school was out for summer. This meant my sister and I would get to spend longer visits with our grandparents. It also meant we'd get to enjoy Granddaddy G's bountiful garden. Grandmama loved fresh strawberries, home-grown tomatoes, fresh peas, and okra. Tall corn stood at attention like saluting soldiers. Everywhere you looked were scrumptious vegetables. There were green peppers, lettuce, and a gazillion cucumbers, ready to be picked and carried inside. Granddaddy G would say, "Grab a little basket, girls. Let's put some fruit and vegetables in it and take it to Grandmama's kitchen." We did as Granddaddy G said because

"It's just better when you do it together.

Eating a meal together at our grandparents' house was very special. You could sneak bites here and there before Grandmama sat down, but you couldn't put your napkin on your lap and really dig in until Granddaddy G prayed, "Lord, thank You for this food and the hands that prepared it. May we keep pure hearts as we try to help others. Use us for Thy service. Amen."

Granddaddy G's prayers were always the same–short, sweet, and to the point. We'd talk and laugh as we sat around the table eating. Granddaddy G would wink at Grandmama and say, "It's just better when you do it together."

Our meal ended with one of Grandmama's yummy desserts. Sometimes it was cobbler. Other times it was cake or scrumptious oatmeal raisin cookies. We'd eat them around the table and then it was time for some family fun–a card game. At some point during the game, bowls of homemade party mix would appear. The edges of the playing cards were marked with our fingerprints because we licked the salt off our fingers. Sometimes we played cards all afternoon and night. Granddaddy's homespun philosophy was right–

"It's just better when you do it together.

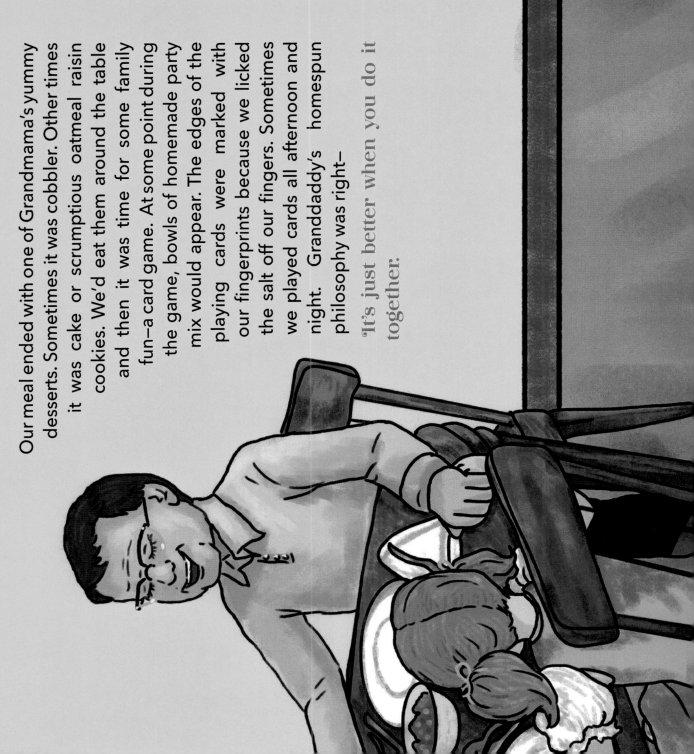

All of these times—sharing meals, playing card games, making the beds, drying dishes, watching TV, gathering berries and vegetables from the garden, road trips and picnics—were wonderful times. They were times that mattered. In fact, they still matter. Some of my most cherished memories are the moments I spent with these special people. And why?

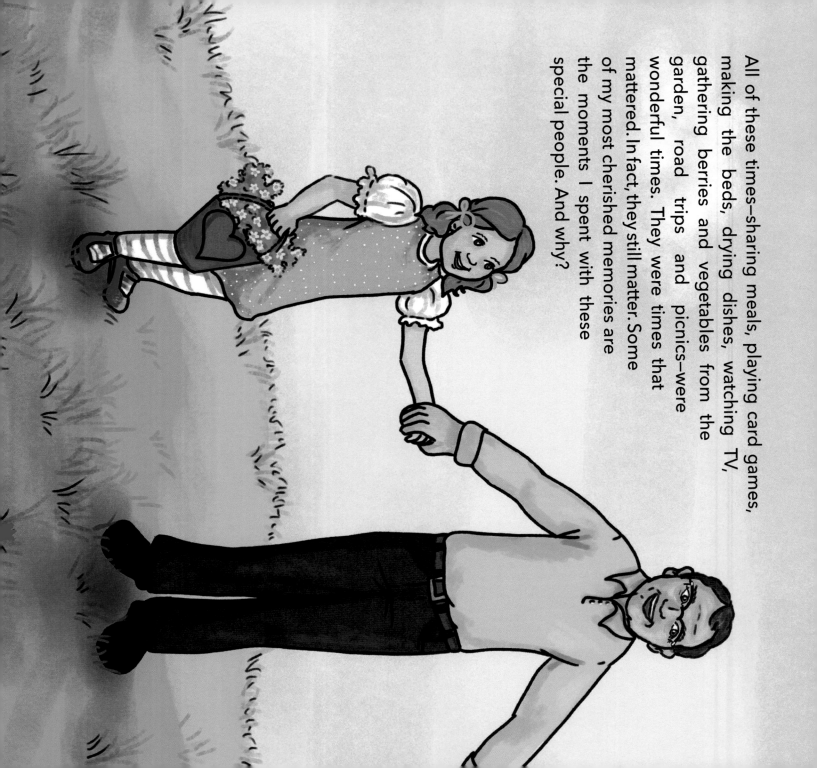

Simply because of Granddaddy G's familiar words that continue to ring in my ears like a comforting chime. They are as soothing as a mother's lullaby. I believe his words are true:

"It's just better when you do it together."

Acknowledgements

To my parents, Don and Carolyn Midgett You are a combination of wit, grace, talent, and charm. Your philosophy is to make the most of each day. Your Faith and your love of God and family is evident to all who know you. Thank you for giving Jenifer and me a childhood full of unconditional love, stability, security, lots of music, singing, fun, family times, and travel. Now that we have families of our own, thank you for planning times for us to all be together, and for loving us all so much. I hope to honor you, as you by example continue to honor your parents, continuing their legacy.

To my big sister, Jenifer Thank you for helping me recall some of our shared cherished childhood memories. Thank you for not thinking I was crazy for wanting to turn our time spent with Grandmama and Granddaddy G into a children's book. Your influence and support as my big sister help me. I love you and your people. I love how Keith brings out your adventurous spirit. Your Hunter, Philine, Mia, Will, and Holly are so special to me. I can't wait to read this book to Mia!

To my husband, Chris Your encouragement and support cannot go unnoticed. Thirty years married to you has gone so fast! Marrying you while you were still in law school, then staying home with our children when they were little, these were not the easiest years. But those choices turned into so many blessings. You have always been an involved, loving father. Together, with intention, our focus stayed on our three children and their interests and activities. Thank you for cheering me on when I returned to graduate school, as I teach, and as I have written this book. I am forever grateful that you knew, loved, and were loved by my grandparents. A high compliment I give to you is when I tell you that you are reminding me of my Granddaddy G, and you "get" with what depth those words from me really mean. You have continued to lead us by example, finding personal strengths and building on those strengths with each opportunity. Building a life with you makes me a better person.

To my older daughter, Allie Your love of learning started when you practiced writing your name at 3 years old over and over just to get your first library card. I am so thankful for the times you had as a little girl with Grandmama and Granddaddy G. Thank you for all your encouragement and help during this book-writing journey. You continue to inspire me in your current role of university professor/writing center director. The love you and **Zach** have for learning and for each other is a beautiful thing. The fact that you have supported each other's dreams through high school, college, law school, graduate school, and your Phd/doctorate years speaks volumes. You are both smart, funny, determined, and kind. I look forward to all you both will do in life as you make a difference in your corner of the world.

To my son, Peyton You have had my heart since the moment you were born. I am thankful you have memories of eating Grandmama G's mashed potatoes and swinging on her swingset with your cousins. Cheering for you from any and every kind of bleacher during many sport seasons through the years has been so fun, and we continue to cheer you on. You are determined, passionate, athletic, and smart. You are the ultimate team player as you try your very best and encourage those around you. You chose well when you chose to marry **Sarai.** You both have the biggest hearts! You and Sarai are such wonderful parents to Emma Kate. You make simple moments opportunities for learning and for fun. I hope you both know I am always on your team.

To my granddaughter, Emma Kate You make me the happiest Netty! Pawpaw and I cannot wait to read this book with you and know soon you will be reading to us. We look forward to watching you grow and learn. I hope to give you many wonderful memories as you grow up. You are an amazing little girl! I hope one day you will read this book to your own children.

To my younger daughter, Elizabeth When you were born, you completed our family nest. I'm so thankful Grandmama G knew you were named for her. She loved reading those little baby board books to you. Elizabeth, you are as beautiful on the inside as you are on the outside. Your patients will be blessed as you care for them and nurse them back to health. Your light has always shone so brightly: keep shining as you do your part to brighten up this world.

Special thanks to Mindy: We both had such wonderful grandparents and anytime we miss them, somehow it helps to talk to each other about it. Sharing our childhood stories has served as a therapy of sorts. I could not have written this book without your friendship and support. You have helped me find my voice.

A note for educators: What an honor it is to be a teacher. My family tree is full of educators, including my grandparents, my mother, and my daughter. First volunteering, and eventually working in the school system, I have been continuously inspired by the educators in our wonderful town. My children received an excellent education and were taught by engaging, empathetic teachers who cared. Our town may be small, but it is full of big-hearted people who devote vast amounts of time and energy to make a difference in the lives of children. I must also add that during graduate school, **Dr. H.** and **Stef E.** helped me broaden my skills, adapt, and grow when I wanted to shy away from new challenges. This is what excellent educators do for their students. I am thankful for my job that I love, surrounded by some of the best people around.

About the Author

Jennette is an enthusiastic elementary school teacher who loves music and books. A mother of three grown children, she realizes the importance of family togetherness. She relates, "Time with family, especially grandparents, is precious time. My own childhood included simple, everyday moments with my grandparents that are some of my best childhood memories."

When Jennette's three children were young, they loved hearing stories about the summers Jennette and her sister Jenifer spent with their grandparents. A believer in life-long learning, Jennette graduated with honors with her master's degree in education curriculum and instruction. An assignment in graduate school sparked the idea to turn her childhood memories into a children's book.

As a teacher, Jennette hopes to remind parents and guardians that time invested in young children is valuable. Jennette shares, "Special moments that become favorite memories for children do not have to be big, elaborate moments. This book is my attempt to use my own story to inspire families with young children to make memories by using everyday moments as opportunities for learning and fun. I hope to encourage family togetherness amongst siblings, extended family, and especially with grandparents. After all, it's just better when you do it together."

Made in the USA
Las Vegas, NV
17 July 2021